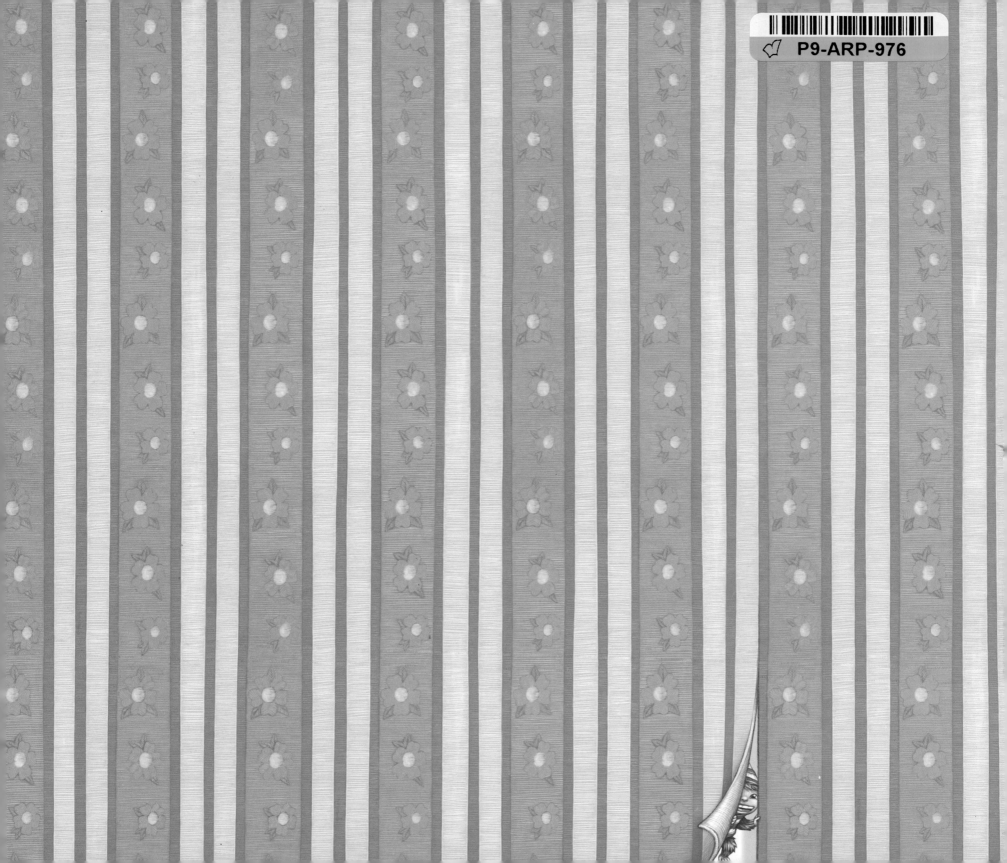

"Keep a watchful eye on the dreamers, for they can transform potted plants into forests, bath water into oceans, and balls of dust into mischievous little creatures..."

—Sir Muffin Muffinsson, the Dream Guardian

For Emma

DUSTRATS!
Or, The Adventures of Sir Muffin Muffinsson

© 2017 by Adrià Regordosa

Published by POW!
a division of powerHouse Packaging & Supply, Inc.
32 Adams Street, Brooklyn, NY 11201-1021

info@powkidsbooks.com • www.powkidsbooks.com
www.powerHouseBooks.com • www.powerHousePackaging.com

Library of Congress Control Number:
2016954879
ISBN: 978-1-57687-821-7
10 9 8 7 6 5 4 3 2 1

Printed in Malaysia

Illustrated

Or, The Adventures of Sir Muffin Muffinsson

Adrià Regordosa

Every night, Sir Muffin stays by Emma's side to keep a close watch on her dreams. Sometimes her dreams can get a little wild.

Lo! Someone must
have forgotten to tidy up
Emma's room this week.
Out from under Emma's crib
pop seven Dustrats,
one for each messy day.
Dustrats love Emma's
extraordinary imagination!

S ir Muffin straps
on his trusty vacuum
and dashes after them.
He'd better nab those
critters before they make
a mess of the whole house.

Monday's Dustrat is gobbling up delicious cookies in the kitchen.

Crumbs everywhere! Brr...why is it so cold in here?

 uesday's Dustrat is snoozing in the living room, that lazybones!

Say, where did all these leaves come from?

 ednesday's Dustrat is rummaging around in the attic. Zooks!

Someone should help that princess, Emma's dream has sharp teeth!

Thursday's Dustrat is swimming around the depths of the bathroom

like a fish. But Sir Muffin hates getting his fur wet.

 riday's Dustrat is snooping in the office. Is Sir Muffin shrinking, or is everything

very tall and important in here? Suddenly Sir Muffin feels as small as a Dustrat.

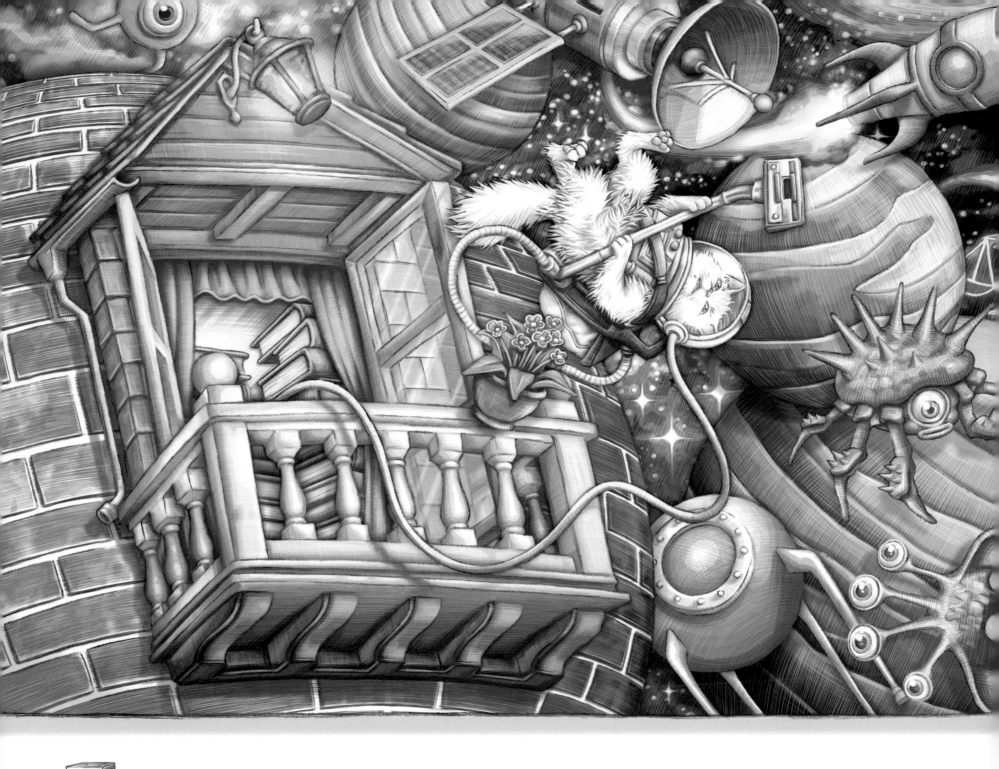

aturday's Dustrat is catching stars outside the window, but that's a bad idea!

Better for a Dustrat to be inside. Inside Sir Muffin's vacuum bag that is.

unday's Dustrat is tinkering in the garage. It sure is spooky in here.

Oh no! Is Emma having a *bad* dream?

Emma!
Has Sir Muffin left
her alone for too long?
Quickly, Sir Muffin,
to the rescue!
Even the Dustrats
are worried.

Zounds! If only Emma's imagination wasn't so wild. How could Sir Muffin have let this happen?

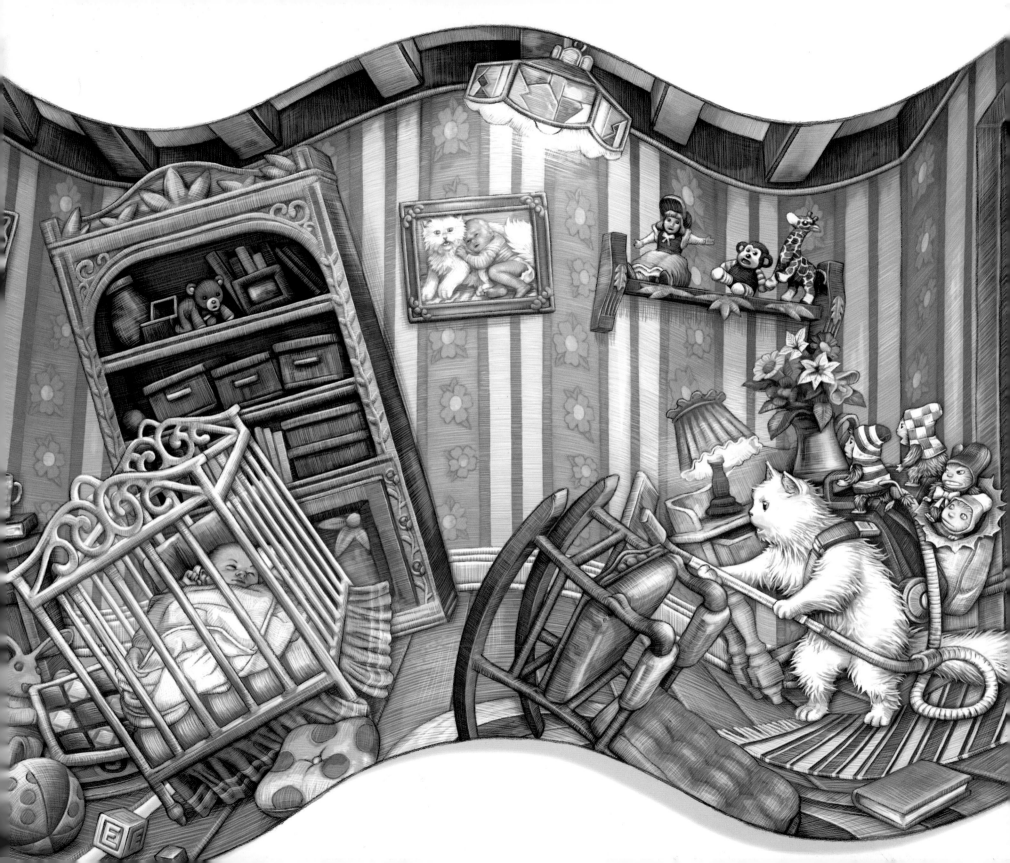

Sir Muffin needs help.

He can't catch Emma on his own!

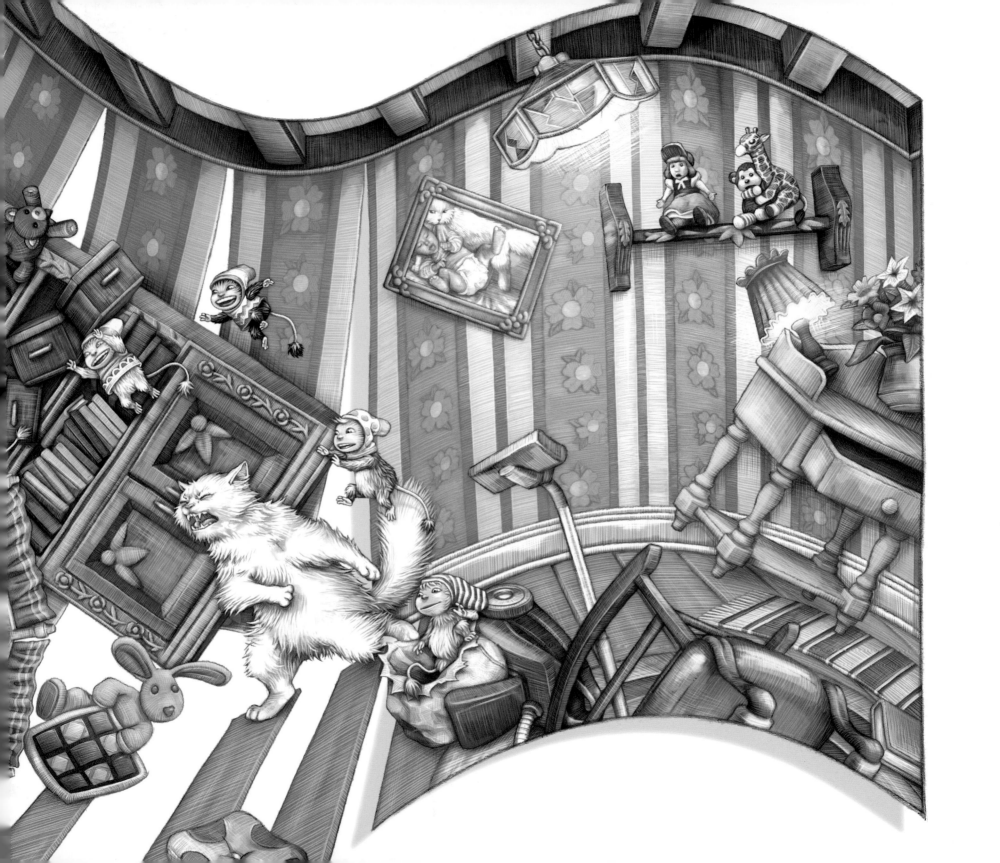

ear not, those clever

Dustrats have an idea.

Together with Sir Muffin,

they've got Emma!

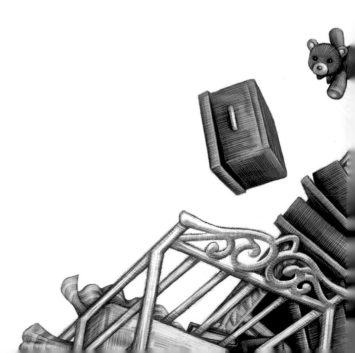

Every night, Sir Muffin and the Dustrats stay by Emma's side to keep a close watch on her dreams. Sometimes her dreams can get a little wild.

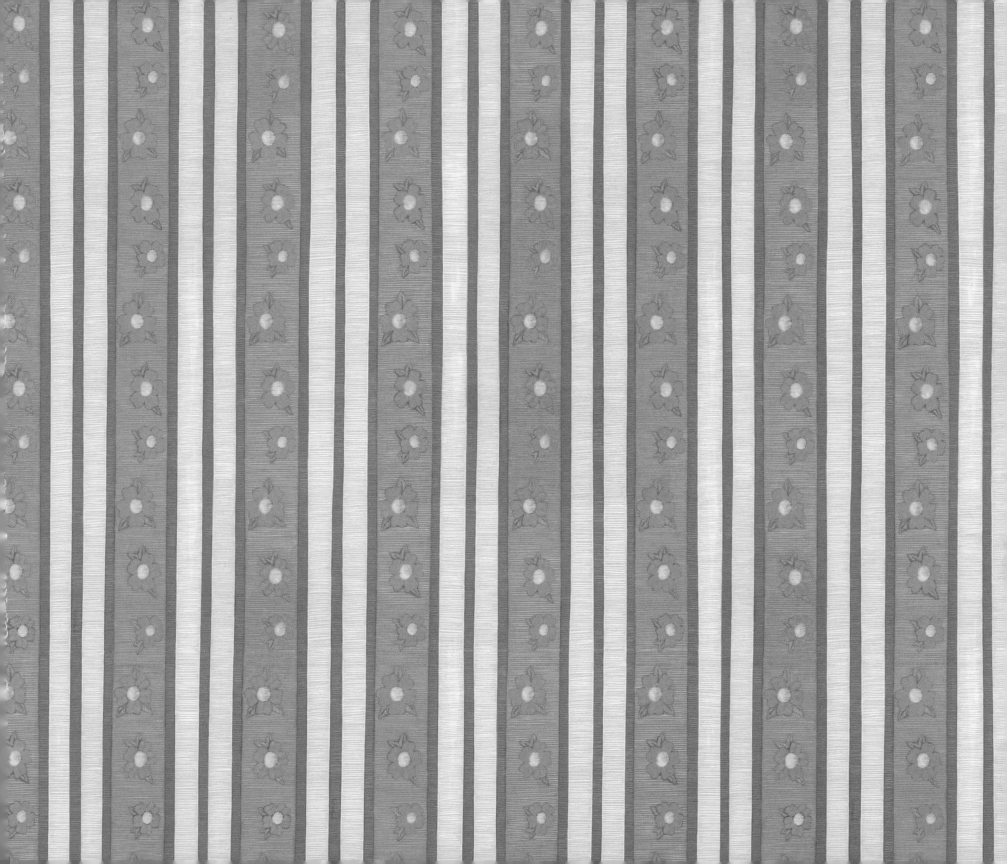